PLEASE WRITE BACK!

To Charlie
—J.M.

Text and illustrations copyright © 2010 by Jennifer E. Morris.

All rights reserved. Published by Scholastic Inc.
SCHOLASTIC, CARTWHEEL BOOKS, and associated logos
are trademarks and/or registered trademarks of Scholastic Inc.
Lexile is a registered trademark of MetaMetrics, Inc.

Library of Congress Cataloging-in-Publication Data

Morris, J. E. (Jennifer E.)
Please write back! / by Jennifer E. Morris.
p. cm. -- (Scholastic reader. Level 1)
Summary: Alfie writes a letter to his grandmother and eagerly
awaits her reply.
ISBN-13: 978-0-545-11506-3 (pbk. : alk. paper)
ISBN-10: 0-545-11506-X (pbk. : alk. paper)
[1. Letters--Fiction. 2. Grandmothers--Fiction.] I. Title. II. Series.

PZ7.M82824Ple 2010
[E]--dc22   2009011176

ISBN: 978-0-545-11506-3

10 9 8 7 6 5 4 3 2 1   10 11 12 13 14/0

Printed in the U.S.A. 40 • First printing, April 2010

PLEASE WRITE BACK!

by Jennifer E. Morris

Cartwheel BOOKS®

SCHOLASTIC INC.
New York Toronto London Auckland
Sydney Mexico City New Delhi Hong Kong

Alfie wrote a letter to Grandma.

Alfie addressed the letter.

He stamped the letter.

And he mailed the letter.

Then he waited for Grandma to write back.

He waited the next day.

And the next day.

And the next day.

But Grandma's letter
did not come.

The next day, Alfie
did not wait for the mail.

"Are you Alfie?" asked
the mailman.

"Do you have a letter for me?" asked Alfie.

"No," said the mailman.

"I have a box."

Inside was a letter.

Dear Alfie,

I love you too!

Love,
Grandma

And a big batch of cookies!
Hooray!

Dear Grandma,

Thank you for the cookies!

Love,
Alfie

"Thank you," said Alfie.

"You're welcome," said Mommy.

"Yes, you may, Alfie," said Mommy.

"Mommy, may I please have a cookie?" he said.

Then Alfie had the best idea of all.

Mommy hugged Alfie.

"Your cookies look yummy.

May I please have one?"

He began to cry.

But he still wanted
a real cookie.

He cut and he colored.

Soon Alfie had his own cookies.

Alfie thought of another idea.
He went to his room and got
some paper.

"Think of a better way
to get a cookie."

"Get down, Alfie!"
cried Mommy.

Then she saw something.

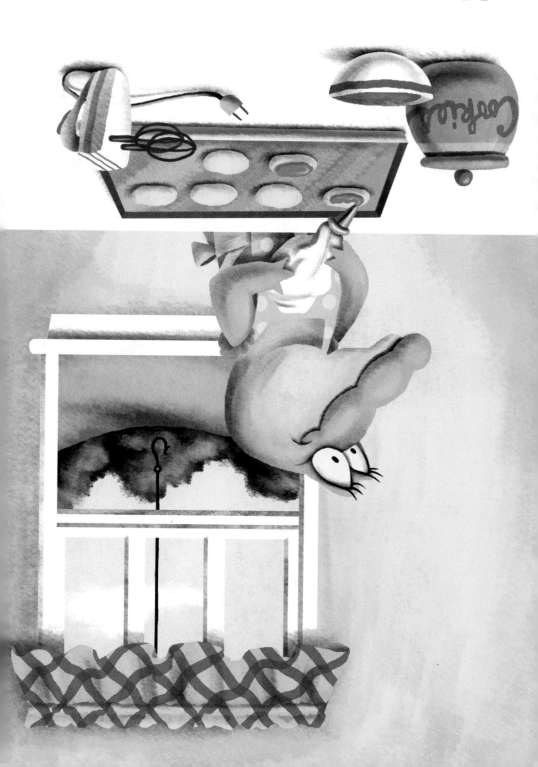

Mommy put icing on the cookies.

Alfie had another idea.

He went outside.

"No, Alfie," said Mommy.
"Think of a better way to get
a cookie."

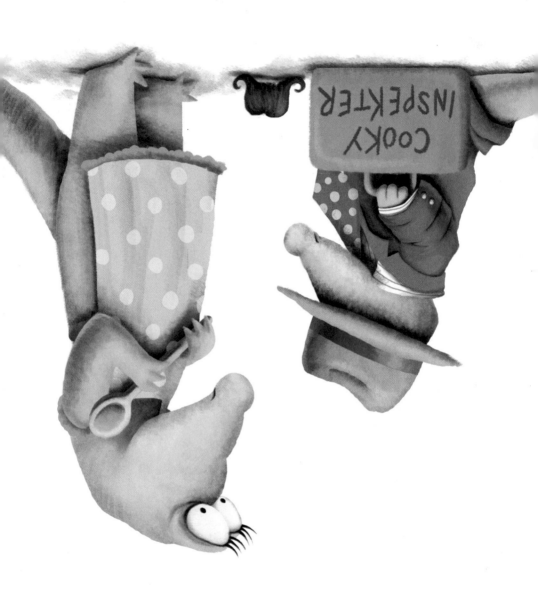

Oops.

"I want a cookie," said Alfie in a big, deep voice.

He found a big coat
and a big hat.

and thought.

Then Alfie got
an idea.

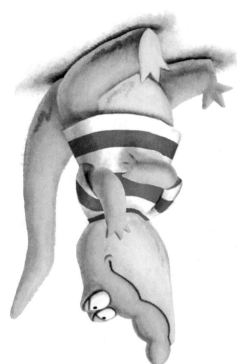

and thought

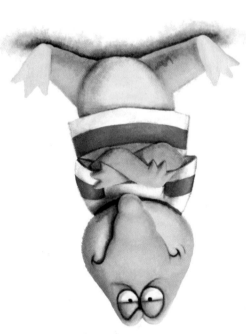

Alfie thought

"Don't grab, Alfie," said Mommy.
"Can you think of a better way
to get a cookie?"

But most of all, Alfie loved to eat cookies.

He loved to look at cookies.

He loved to smell cookies.

Alfie loved cookies.

Mommy was baking cookies.

May I Please Have a Cookie?

SCHOLASTIC READER
LEVEL 1
50-250 WORDS

by Jennifer E. Morris

Cartwheel
·B·O·O·K·S·®

SCHOLASTIC INC.
New York Toronto London Auckland
Sydney Mexico City New Delhi Hong Kong

To Robin and Leo
—J.M.

No part of this publication may be reproduced, stored in a retrieval system, or transmitted in any form or by any means, electronic, mechanical, photocopying, recording, or otherwise, without written permission of the publisher. For information regarding permission, write to Scholastic Inc., Attention: Permissions Department, 557 Broadway, New York, NY 10012.

Copyright © 2005 by Jennifer Morris.

All rights reserved. Published by Scholastic Inc.
SCHOLASTIC, CARTWHEEL BOOKS, and associated logos
are trademarks and/or registered trademarks of Scholastic Inc.
Lexile is a registered trademark of MetaMetrics, Inc.

Library of Congress Cataloging-in-Publication Data
Morris, J. E. (Jennifer E.)
  May I please have a cookie? / by J.E. Morris
    p. cm.
  "Cartwheel books."
  Summary: Alfie, a young alligator, learns the best way to ask for a
cookie from his mother.
  ISBN 0-439-73819-9
  [1. Etiquette — Fiction. 2. Alligators — Fiction. 3. Cookies — Fiction] I. Title.
  PZ7.M82824Ma 2005
  [E] — dc22   2004031113

ISBN-13: 978-0-439-73819-4
ISBN-10: 0-439-73819-9

10 9 8 7 6 5 4 3 2 1   09 10 11 12

Printed in the U.S.A. 40 • This edition first printing, September 2008

May I Please Have a Cookie?